It's a YUMee world

Aoileann Garavaglia

It's a YuMee world

Aoileann Garavaglia

BLACKWATER PRESS

Dedication

To all young testers and tasters. Enjoy YUMee treats.

Said by Aoileann While Eating a Giant Icicle, Collected from Beneath a Gorse Growing Alongside the Road in Glencree

'I'd love it if God made orange rain.'
Linda Garavaglia, winter 1974

Editor
Sinéad Lawton

Design/Cover
Melanie Gradtke

Illustrations
Bronagh O'Hanlon
Anne Honermann

©2002 Aoileann Garavaglia
ISBN 1-84131-586-9

Produced in Ireland by
Blackwater Press
c/o Folens Publishers
Hibernian Industrial Estate
Greenhills Road
Tallaght, Dublin 24

Contents

Aknowledgements

I wish to thank the team involved in making this book:
my editors Margaret Burns and Sinéad Lawton for their
enthusiasm and patience, Melanie Gradtke for the design,
Bronagh O'Hanlon and Anne Honermann for their visual
humour, Nicola Webster for the cover photo and
John O'Connor for taking on the project.

This also gives me the opportunity to show my appreciation
for the wonderful support I received in making the TV series
It's a YUMee World. Grazie to Kevin Linehan, Tony McHugh,
John Keogh, Alan Robinson, Gary Mitchel of CEL and all my colleagues in the Young
People's Department of RTÉ. Thank you also to Simone Delaney for the set design,
Shirley Dalton for the graphic design, Marie Dorgan and Patricia Masterson for their
much appreciated helping hand in the kitchen, and to all the crews with which I
worked.

A big go raibh míle maith agat to John Williams, series producer of *YUMee*, who
helped devise the series.

A special thank you to Sheila Rasmussen, food advisor, for her hard work, advice and
friendship.

A big thank you also to friends and family: Mum, Papa, Caoimhín, Grannies, Kathleen
Morris and family, Beek Grosh and family, Kari Rocca and family, Mary Kingston and
Brian Graham, Francois Drion and family, Richard Carragher and family and Mary
and all the Clonakilty Barretts, without whose loving friendship and support this book
would never have happened.

By the way, a big thank you to all above for being the best testers and tasters.

Cookery Terms

Here are some words used in cookery that you may find in this book. If there is a word that you don't understand when you read a recipe, check back to this page.

Beat
Mix together by stirring very hard with a fork or whisk.

Blend
Make something into a smooth paste, usually in an electric blender.

Cream
Mix butter or margarine with sugar into a creamy mixture with a wooden spoon.

Fold in
Mix two things using a gentle slicing/turning movement with a wooden spoon.

Knead
Squeeze and stretch dough to make it ready for baking.

Rub in
Mix butter or margarine with flour by rubbing them with your fingertips.

Whisk
Add air by beating very fast with a hand whisk.

Sieve
Pass ingredients through a sieve to get any lumps out using a teaspoon.

Pestle and mortar
A club-shaped tool and bowl, made out of a hard material like wood or stone, used to crush ingredients.

Weights, Measures and Servings

Sometimes you may have a weighing scales or measuring jug that measure things out in a different way than is done in this book. If you do, ask a grown-up to help you to work out how much you need of something from the chart below.

Solids		Liquids	
Metric	Imperial	Metric	Imperial
15g	½ oz	5ml	1 teaspoon
30g	1oz	15ml	1 tablespoon
50g	1⅔ oz	150ml	¼ pint
150g	5oz	300ml	½ pint
300g	10oz	600ml	1 pint
480g	16oz (1lb)	1 litre	1¾ pints
720g	1½ lb	1.1 litres	2 pints
1kg	2lb 1⅓ oz	250ml	1 cup

- Always use weighing scales to weigh amounts carefully.
- A 'pinch' of salt or pepper is the amount you can hold between your thumb and first finger.
- When you measure with spoons they should be level, not heaped. A good trick is to fill the spoon and then level it off using the edge of a table knife.

Oven Temperatures

All ovens are different and cooking times are only a guide. Get into the habit of touching and looking at food to find out if it is properly cooked.

Gas Mark	Centigrade	Fahrenheit	
¼	80°C	175°F	Cool
½	110°C	225°F	
1	130°C	250°F	
2	150°C	300°F	
3	170°C	325°F	Moderate
4	180°C	350°F	
5	190°C	375°F	
6	200°C	400°F	
7	220°C	425°F	Hot
8	230°C	450°F	**Very Hot**

NEVER USE AN OVEN, COOKER OR MICROWAVE WITHOUT THE HELP OF AN ADULT.

Kitchen Safety

The recipes in this book were written for you, but it is always a good idea to show the recipe to a grown-up before you start to cook.

- Always let a grown-up know when you are going to work in the kitchen.
- Always wear an apron or smock before you start to cook, to protect your clothing and for safety. Tie your hair back if you need to.
- Clear a work area before you start.
- Read the whole recipe through to make sure you have all the ingredients and tools.
- Wash your hands with soap and water before and after you handle food.
- Never use sharp knives. Always use a table knife and have a grown-up with you while you use a knife. If you have any difficulties, ask an adult to cut the ingredients for you.
- Always wear an oven glove if you are going to handle hot dishes.
- Wash all fruit and vegetables.
- Never taste with your fingers, use a spoon.
- Leave enough time to cook and clean up.
- Clean up spills and crumbs on the counter and floor. Always use a clean cloth when wiping counters.
- Put all the extra ingredients away.
- Make sure the adult checks to see if the oven, grill, cooker and microwave are switched off.

Leave the kitchen clean and tidy.

Kitchen Safety

A grown-up must always be present if you are using the cooker.

A grown-up must always be present if you are using the microwave. Beware, because containers are deceptively hot.

A grown-up must always be present when you are using the oven. Ask the grown-up to help you preheat the oven and to help you put dishes in to cook and take them out again when they are ready.

Always ask a grown-up to help you if you are going to use a blender.

Some of the recipes in this book contain nuts. Some people are allergic to nuts and aren't allowed to eat them. Ask an adult if it is safe for you to eat nuts. If nuts are used in a recipe you will see this symbol.

Cookery Tips

Here are some tips you will find useful as you follow the recipes in this book and in cooking generally.

Separating an egg
Gently crack the egg onto a saucer. Place an eggcup over the yolk to trap it and carefully pour the egg white into a bowl. Hey presto! The egg white has been separated from the egg yolk.

Greasing tins
To stop food sticking in the tin, wipe all over the inside of the tin with a paper towel dipped in margarine.

To line a 10-inch cake tin
Get a large piece of baking paper. Place your cake tin upside down on the paper and draw around the rim using a pencil. Cut out the circle you have drawn with your safety scissors. Cut two strips of baking paper about 15cm wide and 40cm long. Fold the strips in half along the length. Make cuts along the length about 5cm apart to the centre fold. Put the uncut parts of the strips against the inside wall of the cake tin, with the cut part of the strips on the bottom of the tin. Place the circular piece of paper over the cut part of the strips. The bottom and inside wall of the cake tin should now be lined with baking paper. This will stop the cake from sticking to the tin, and make it easy to remove.

Sticky tin (tip for non-cook cakes)
Struggling while trying to get the No Bake Belgian Chocolate Cake out of the tin? There must be an easier way! Here's a great tip. Before you empty the mixture into the tin, line the tin with some cling film and the cake will just lift out.

Eyes watery?
When you chop onions and spring onions, they can make your eyes water. Try rinsing them in cold water before you start chopping them.
Always wash your hands after chopping garlic or onions and don't put your fingers near your mouth or eyes because the juice from the garlic or onion can sting.

Making pastry

A secret to good pastry is the less you have to handle it the better it turns out.

Take your time!

When mixing things together, it is worth your while to take your time and mix everything really well.

Save time!

When making dressings or sauces, double the amounts and store in a jar in the fridge for another time.

Don't have a cookie cutter?

If you don't have cookie cutters, you could always use the rim of a glass or cup, just dip it in a little flour first.

Butter too hard?

Put the butter into a small mixing bowl and leave it to sit out at room temperature to soften.

Food too hot?

If you are baking something in an oven, it is a good idea to leave it aside to cool for a little while before you eat.

Spoon all sticky?

If you find it tricky to get golden syrup off a spoon, here's a great tip. Dip the spoon into some warm water before you scoop out the golden syrup and the syrup will slide off the spoon.

Posh Scones

Best eaten within a couple of hours of making them.

To make 12 scones you will need

225g self-raising flour
75g butter
1 egg
100ml milk
50g sultanas
1 tablespoon white sugar

Tools

table knife
small mixing bowl
weighing scales
sieve
large mixing bowl
wooden spoon
rolling pin
a glass
measuring jug
non-stick baking tray
chopping board
teaspoon
fork

1 Sieve the flour into a large mixing bowl using a teaspoon.

2 Add the sugar to the flour.

3 Use a table knife to chop the butter into little pieces. Using the tips of your fingers, rub the butter into the sugar and flour until it feels all crumbly.

4 Add the sultanas.

5 In a separate bowl, beat the egg and milk together with a fork.

YUMee 14

6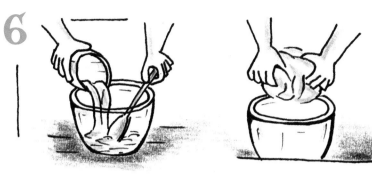

Pour the egg and milk mixture into the flour, butter and sugar, and mix well using a wooden spoon until it becomes too stiff to mix. Use your hands to form a dough ball.

7

On a large floured chopping board, roll out the dough using a rolling pin. Leave the dough about 2cm thick.

8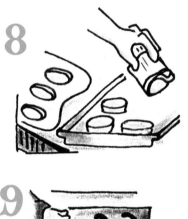

Cut out individual scones using the rim of a glass. Place the scones on a non-stick baking tray. After you have cut out the first few, just roll the dough out again and cut out the rest.

9

Ask a grown-up to preheat the oven to a moderate temperature, 190°C/375°F/gas mark 5. Bake the scones in the oven for about 12–15minutes.

Serve with cream and jam.

Beach Breaky Bickies

To make about 25 Bickies you will need

100g white sugar
175g butter
175g soft brown sugar
75g plain white flour
225g porridge oats
1 egg
2 tablespoons water
1 tablespoon vanilla essence
1 teaspoon cinnamon

Tools

weighing scales
large mixing bowl
wooden spoon
tablespoon
teaspoon
sieve
2 non-stick baking trays
wire rack

1

Add the white sugar to the butter and give them a good mix using a wooden spoon. The mixture should become thick and creamy with no lumps.

2

Mix the egg in with the butter and sugar.

3

Add the water, vanilla essence, cinnamon and brown sugar and mix well.

4

Sieve in the flour and keep mixing.

5

Add the oats a little at a time and mix well.

6

For each Bicky, scoop 1 tablespoon of the mixture onto a non-stick baking tray. Mash it down a little with the back of the spoon. Leave some space between each Bicky as they will spread out as they cook. You will be able to fit about half the mixture onto each tray.

7

Ask a grown-up to help preheat the oven to a moderate temperature, 180°C/350°F/gas mark 4. Bake the Bickies for about 15 minutes. The cooking time depends on the thickness of the Bickies, the thicker the Bicky, the longer it takes to cook.

8

Ask a grown-up to help you place the Bickies on a wire rack to cool, this will make them nice and crispy.

Best served with a nice glass of milk or some OJ.

No Bake Belgian Chocolate Cake

Keep a couple of marshmallows to stick on the top.

You will need

200g digestive biscuits
225g dark chocolate
50g butter
125ml whipped cream
200g/1 packet large
    marshmallows
50g pecan nuts

Tools

measuring jug
large mixing bowl
bowl that can go in the
    microwave
non-stick, round 8-inch cake tin
chopping board
table knife
whisk
wooden spoon
dessertspoon
spatula
weighing scales

1

Melt the chocolate and butter in the microwave at a low heat for about 3 minutes.

2

In a large mixing bowl, whisk the cream until it becomes thick.

3

Break up the biscuits into large chunks and add these to the cream.

4

Add the marshmallows and pecan nuts to the biscuits and cream, and fold everything together using a wooden spoon.

Serve with vanilla ice-cream or just a large glass of milk.

5
Pour the melted chocolate and butter into the cream and biscuit mixture, and mix well.

6
Scoop the mixture into a non-stick cake tin and, using the back of a dessertspoon, mash it into the tin. Really pack it in.

7
Stick the extra marshmallows on the top and place the cake in the fridge for 4 hours. It might be a good idea to leave it overnight.

8
Remove the cake from the fridge, using a spatula to prise around the edges to loosen it from the tin. Then tip the cake out onto a board. Use a table knife to slice.

Garlic Bread

1 Cut the bread into slices using a table knife on a clean breadboard.

2 Chop the parsley using a table knife on a clean chopping board. Put the butter in a mixing bowl and add the parsley.

You will need
50g butter
1 small clove of garlic
a handful of parsley
1 long Italian or French stick
salt and pepper

Tools
weighing scales
breadboard
chopping board
table knife
mixing bowl
garlic crusher
fork
baking tray
tin foil
serving plate/party platter

Buon Appetito

YUMee 20

3

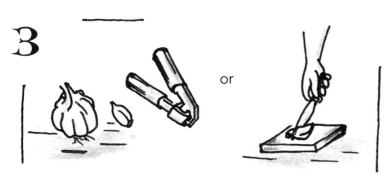 or

Get a grown-up to help you crush a clove of garlic. Use a garlic crusher if you have one, or you can chop the garlic with a table knife.

4

Add the garlic to the butter and parsley and use a fork to mix it all together.

5

Spread the butter onto both sides of each slice of bread using a table knife. Season with a little salt and pepper.

6

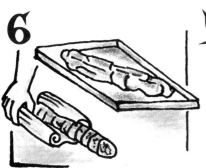

Assemble all the slices back into the shape of the French stick and loosely wrap it in foil. Place the bread onto a baking tray.

7

Ask a grown-up to preheat the oven to a moderate to hot temperature, 190°C/ 375°F/gas mark 5. Bake for about 20 minutes.

8

When your garlic bread is cooked, get a grown-up to remove the foil and place the bread onto a plate or party platter.

21 YUMee

Noodle Oodle

You will need

For the noodles
1 packet of
    ready-to-make egg noodles
1 red pepper
1 yellow pepper
3 green spring onions
1 small box of bean sprouts

For the dressing
1 tablespoon olive oil
2 tablespoons sesame seed oil
1 tablespoon light soy sauce
1 teaspoon mustard
1 teaspoon maple syrup

To garnish
a little chopped parsley and
    chopped coriander

Tools
chopping board
table knife
2 tablespoons
teaspoon
large mixing bowl/salad bowl
colander
clean jam jar with lid

1

Put all of the ingredients for the dressing into a clean jam jar. Put the lid on tightly and give it a good shake.

2

On a chopping board, cut the top off the red and yellow peppers using your table knife. Cut the peppers in half and remove the seeds. Rinse the peppers under a cold tap and then use a table knife to cut them into little strips.

3

Put the bean sprouts into a colander and rinse under the cold tap.

4

Using a table knife and chopping board, carefully chop the green onions into little bits.

5

Ask a grown-up to help you follow the instructions on the packet to heat up your noodles. Some noodles are precooked and only need to be heated in a microwave.

6

Put the noodles into a large bowl. Add in the peppers, bean sprouts, green onions and dressing. Fold well using two tablespoons.

7

Garnish with a little chopped parsley and chopped coriander or even with just a little more chopped pepper.

In China and other Asian countries, it is a custom to eat noodles on your birthday because long noodles are believed to mean that you will live a long life.

Try eating with chopsticks. Chi Bao

23 YUM

Brownies

Great idea for a party or even a birthday cake.

To make about 24 Brownies you will need

125g butter
125g dark chocolate
    (70% pure coco)
2 eggs
175g white sugar
1 teaspoon vanilla essence
125g plain white flour
1 teaspoon baking powder
75g chopped walnuts
coloured sweets to decorate

Tools

2 large mixing bowls
weighing scales, whisk
wooden spoon, teaspoon
tablespoon, sieve, table knife
non-stick baking tray
baking paper

1

Put the chocolate and butter into a mixing bowl. With the help of a grown-up, melt them in the microwave at a low heat for about 3 minutes.

2

In another mixing bowl, whisk the eggs and then gradually add the sugar, whisking all the time.

3

Add the melted chocolate and butter to the egg mixture, constantly stirring with a wooden spoon.

4

Add in the vanilla essence.

5

Sieve the flour and baking powder into the chocolate mixture and mix with a wooden spoon.

6

Add in the walnuts and stir with the wooden spoon.

7

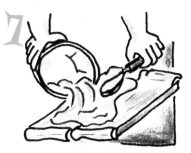

Line a baking tray with baking paper. Pour the mixture into the baking tray and spread it about with the back of a tablespoon.

8

Ask a grown-up to preheat the oven to a moderate temperature, 180°C/350°F/gas mark 4. Bake for about 20 minutes and, while they are still a little warm, cut your Brownies into squares with a table knife.

9

Decorate each square with coloured sweets.

Serve with a nice big cold glass of milk.

Cardamom Seed Cake

You will need

300g plain white flour
2 teaspoons baking powder
100g butter
175g sugar
1½ teaspoons crushed
    cardamom (24 pods)
1 egg
175ml milk
some crystal sugar to decorate

Tools

pestle and mortar
sieve
large mixing bowl
weighing scales
large measuring jug
table knife
wooden spoon
teaspoon
non-stick 10-inch cake tin
    with a hole in the middle
chopping board

1 Remove the cardamom seeds from their pods and crush them using a pestle and mortar, getting a grown-up to help you.

2 Sieve the flour and baking powder into a large mixing bowl.

3

Chop the butter into small chunks and then add them to the bowl. Use your fingers to work the butter into the flour until it turns into crumbs.

4

Add in the sugar and the crushed cardamom.

5

Mix the egg and milk in a large measuring jug.

6

Add the milk and egg to the flour mixture and mix well with a wooden spoon.

7

Pour the mixture into the cake tin, wiping any spills with a wet cloth.

8

Ask a grown-up to preheat the oven to a moderate temperature, 180°C/350°F/gas mark 4. Bake your cake in the oven for about 30–35 minutes. Leave it aside to cool when cooked.

You can always use ground cardamom which is available in most supermarkets.

9

Decorate with some crystal sugar.

Sprinkle the top with coconut or grated chocolate.

Eskimo Ices

To make about 24 Eskimo Ices you will need

For the white chocolate
100g white chocolate
200ml evaporated milk
150ml cream

For the dark chocolate
100g dark chocolate
    (70% coco)
200ml evaporated milk
150ml cream

fruit to decorate

Tools
weighing scales
bowl that can go in the
    microwave
large Pyrex measuring jug
wooden spoon
mould
    (or small glasses or tea cups)
serving plate, tin opener

1 Get a grown-up to help you melt the white chocolate in the microwave for about 3 minutes at a low heat.

2 Stir the cream and evaporated milk in a large jug. Add in the melted white chocolate and mix well.

3 Half fill the mould with the white chocolate mixture, leaving enough space for the dark chocolate to go on top.

4 Place the mould in the freezer for a couple of hours to let the white chocolate base set.

5 Make the dark chocolate topping in the same way.

6 Pour the dark chocolate on top of the white chocolate. Place the mould back in the freezer. It is best to leave it overnight.

7 Remove from the freezer. Press the Eskimo Ices out of the mould onto a plate and decorate with fruit. If you made them in a glass or tea cup, decorate the top with some fruit and serve in the glass/cup with a spoon. They are easy to spoon out.

29 YUMee

You will need

125g butter
250g white sugar
2 eggs
300g white flour
2½ teaspoons baking powder
1 teaspoon salt
250ml milk
½ teaspoon vanilla essence

To decorate

icing sugar
birthday candles

Tools

large mixing bowl
weighing scales
sieve
wooden spoon
teaspoon
measuring jug
10-inch cake tin
baking paper

YUMee Birthday Cake

(Best Birthday Cake)

1

Put the butter into a mixing bowl and leave it to sit out at room temperature for about half an hour until it becomes soft. Add in the sugar and give them a good mix using a wooden spoon. The mixture should become thick and creamy with no lumps.

2

Add the eggs to the creamed butter and sugar and mix well.

3

Add in the vanilla essence and the milk and mix well.

4

Sieve in the flour and baking powder. Add the salt and mix with a wooden spoon.

5

Line a cake tin with baking paper.

6

Ask a grown-up to preheat the oven to a moderate temperature 180°C/ 350°F/gas mark 4. Bake in the oven for about 40–50 minutes. After your cake has cooked leave it to cool for about 30 minutes. This really helps it set.

7

Decorate with some icing sugar and birthday candles.

Lá breithe faoi shonas dhuit.

HAPPY BIRTHDAY

Couscous

Great for a light tea, lunch or snack.

You will need

200g couscous
250ml hot water
½ chicken or vegetable
    stock cube
a red, a green and
    a yellow pepper
1 red onion
4 tablespoons olive oil
handful of parsley
handful of mint
handful of basil
salt and pepper
1 small clove of garlic

To garnish

some extra herbs

Tools

weighing scales
2 large mixing bowls
chopping board
table knife
garlic crusher
roasting dish
large Pyrex measuring jug
tablespoon
fork

To prepare the vegetables

1

Wash all the peppers, remove the seeds from the inside and cut them into large chunks using a table knife. Put the chunks of pepper into a large mixing bowl.

2

Peel the red onion and chop it into large chunks and add these to the peppers.

3

Wash and chop the parsley, mint and basil and add these to the peppers and onion.

4

Using a garlic crusher and with the help of a grown-up, crush the clove of garlic. Add the garlic to the other vegetables. Pour 3 tablespoons of olive oil over the vegetables and mix well, coating all the vegetables with olive oil. Season with salt and pepper.

While the vegetables are roasting

7

Ask a grown-up to measure the hot water in a measuring jug and dissolve ½ stock cube in the water.

5

Pour the vegetables into a roasting dish.

6

Ask a grown-up to preheat the oven to a moderate temperature, 200°C/ 400°F/gas mark 6. Roast the vegetables for about 20 minutes. Once cooked, leave aside to cool a little.

8

Pour the couscous into a mixing bowl. Pour the stock slowly over the couscous and use a fork to fluff it up. Watch it swell! It should take about 10 minutes for the couscous to soak up all the lovely juices. Add a tablespoon of olive oil and some salt and pepper to the couscous and mix well.

9

Pour the vegetables on top of the couscous and serve.

MAP

Garnish with some extra herbs and serve warm.

Serve with a nice glass of milk.

To make about 24 Muffins you will need

100g light brown sugar
175ml sunflower oil
2 eggs
225g plain white flour
2 teaspoons baking powder
1 teaspoon cinnamon
zest of ½ orange
2 medium carrots

Tools

2 large mixing bowls
weighing scales
whisk
grater, sieve
wooden spoon
fork
tablespoon, teaspoon
cupcake baking tray
paper cupcake cases

Carrot and Orange Muffins

1 In a large mixing bowl, beat the oil and sugar together using a whisk.

2 Beat the eggs in a separate bowl.

3 Add the eggs to the oil and sugar, and whisk.

4 Sieve the flour and baking powder into the oil, sugar and eggs.

5

Ask a grown-up to help you grate the orange zest and the carrots. Add the cinnamon, orange zest and carrots to your mixture. Mix all the ingredients together using a wooden spoon. Line a cupcake baking tray with paper cases. Spoon some mixture into each paper case. If you have any spills, wipe them using a damp cloth.

6

Ask a grown-up to preheat the oven to a moderate to hot temperature, 200°C/ 400°F/gas mark 6. Bake your muffins for about 15–20 minutes. Leave them to cool once they come out of the oven.

To make the icing, see the Tea Party Menu, page 64.

Repeat the filling ingredients and steps for the other half of the dough.

Danish Pastries

Great idea for breakfast after a slumber party.

You will need

For the dough
(to make 24 pastries)

250g plain white flour
2 teaspoons/1 sachet dried yeast
2 tablespoons sugar
100ml warm milk
50g butter
1 egg

For the filling
(enough for 12 pastries)

1 egg
1 tablespoon milk
2 teaspoons cinnamon
4 teaspoons sugar
1 cup raisins

Tools

large mixing bowl
small mixing bowl
weighing scales
baking tray, baking paper
wooden spoon, cling film
rolling pin, tablespoon
pastry brush, table knife
chopping board
measuring jug
teaspoon
fork

To make the dough

1 Stir the yeast, 1 tablespoon of sugar and the warm milk in the large mixing bowl. Mix well to dissolve the yeast.

2 In a separate bowl, beat the egg with a fork. Add the egg to the yeast, sugar and milk.

3 Melt the butter in the microwave at a low heat for about 3 minutes, and add this to the yeast mixture.

4 Add the flour and 1 tablespoon of sugar to your mixture. Use your hands to mix.

5

Knead the bread in the bowl using your knuckles. Once you have formed a dough ball, remove it from the bowl and continue to knead for about 5 minutes on a flat work surface using some flour to stop it from sticking.

6

Place the dough back in the bowl, cover with cling film and leave it to sit in a warm place for about 2 hours. Watch it rise!!!

7

Once the dough has risen, remove the cling film and give the dough in the bowl a few good punches to knock out all the air.

8

Break the dough ball in half. Roll one half flat on a floured surface until it is about 2cm thick. Add flour if you find it too sticky.

12

Line a baking tray with baking paper and place each Danish on it. Brush the top of each Danish with a little egg and milk.

To make the filling

9

Beat the egg and milk together.

11

10

Brush the dough with the egg and milk, sprinkle on the cinnamon and sugar and scatter a handful of raisins over the top.

Roll it up into one long roll. Use a table knife to cut into little Danish Pastries.

13

Ask a grown-up to preheat the oven to a moderate temperature, 190°C/375°F/gas mark 5. Bake for about 10–15 minutes, depending on the size of your pastries.

Nachos Muchos Grandes

To make the salsa

You will need

For the nachos

1 large packet of tortilla chips
1 tin of red kidney beans
50g chopped cheddar cheese
a red and a green pepper

For the salsa

2 vine ripe tomatoes
1 small red onion
1 cup coriander
½ lime
½ teaspoon white sugar
salt and pepper

Tools

mixing bowl
chopping board
juicer
baking tray, tin foil
party platter/large plate
table knife
tablespoon, teaspoon
tin opener
sieve

1

Chop up the tomatoes with a table knife on a clean chopping board. Put the chopped tomatoes into a mixing bowl.

2

Chop the red onion into small pieces and add to the tomatoes.

3

Using a juicer, squeeze the lime. Add the juice, sugar and a little salt and pepper to the bowl.

4

Chop the coriander with a table knife and add to the bowl. Mix well and leave the mixture to sit for about an hour. The longer your salsa sits, the better it will taste as all the flavours will have had time to combine together.

To prepare the nachos

5 Line a baking tray with tin foil. Pour the tortilla chips into the baking tray and spread them about.

6 Get a grown-up to help you open the tin of kidney beans. Drain off the juice by straining them through a sieve over the sink.

7 Wash and chop the red and green peppers using a table knife.

8 Sprinkle the chips with some kidney beans and chopped red and green pepper. Top it off with the chopped cheese.

9 Ask a grown-up to preheat the oven to a moderate temperature 180°C/ 350°F/gas mark 4. Bake the Nachos Muchos Grandes in the oven for about 10 minutes or until all the cheese is melted.

10 When your nachos are cooked, ask a grown-up to remove them from the baking tray and put them on a party platter.

11 Pour a good amount of salsa on top of the nachos using a tablespoon.

Dilo con nachos

Serve with some fruit punch for a Mexican fiesta party.

39 YUMee

Try any other topping you like. These are a great idea for a party.

Tapas

To make about 15 Tapas you will need

For the base
1 French stick

3 tablespoons olive oil (and a little to coat)

For the toppings
a little red pepper

some cheddar cheese

sliced apple

salami

1 egg

1 tablespoon mayonnaise

salt and pepper

Tools
tablespoon

breadboard

table knife

non-stick baking tray

small mixing bowl

small cookie cutters

chopping board

To make the base

1 Carefully cut the French stick into slices on a clean breadboard.

2 Pour the olive oil into a non-stick baking tray.

3 Place the sliced bread onto the baking tray and coat each piece with olive oil on both sides.

4 Ask a grown-up to preheat the oven to a hot temperature, 220°C/425°F/gas mark 7. Cook the bread slices in the oven for about 10 minutes or until golden brown, be careful not to burn them. Once the bread is cooked, leave aside to cool and become crispy.

To make the toppings

5

Ask a grown-up to hard boil the egg for you. Peel the egg and chop it using a table knife and put it in a bowl. Add in the mayonnaise, a pinch of salt and pepper and mix well. Wash some red pepper and chop using a table knife. Use the egg mayonnaise and pepper as one topping.

6

Try cheddar cheese and sliced apple as another topping or, for party tapas, cut out shapes in the cheese and salami using small cookie cutters.

Feliz cocina

Jungle Yam Yams

To make about 20 Yam Yams you will need

For the yam yams
100g butter
125g white sugar
1 teaspoon ground nutmeg
1 egg
rind of 1 lemon
1 teaspoon baking powder
1 sweet potato
350g flour

To decorate
200g icing sugar
1 tablespoon lemon juice
1½ tablespoons water

Tools
animal biscuit cutters
large mixing bowl
weighing scales
wooden spoon, table spoon
teaspoon
table knife
grater
potato peeler
sieve, wire rack
rolling pin
baking tray
baking paper

For a taste of Africa or a tummy rumble in the jungle try these delicious Jungle Yam Yams. Great for parties.

1 Add the sugar to the butter in a large mixing bowl and give them a good mix using a wooden spoon. The mixture should become thick and creamy with no lumps.

2 Add the egg to the creamed butter and sugar and mix.

3 Get a grown-up to help you peel and grate the sweet potato and grate the rind of a lemon. Add them to the creamed butter and sugar.

4 Sieve in the flour, baking powder and nutmeg and mix well.

5

Form the mixture into a dough ball. Roll the dough out on a floured surface with a rolling pin until it is about 2cm thick.

6

Cut out individual biscuits using cookie cutters.

7

Line a baking tray with baking paper and place the biscuits on the baking tray.

Hakuna Matata

8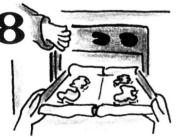

Ask a grown-up to preheat the oven to a moderate temperature, 180°C/ 350°F/ gas mark 4. Bake the Yam Yams in the oven for about 10–12 minutes, depending on the thickness.

9

Ask a grown-up to help you place the Yam Yams on a wire rack to cool before you eat them.

10

Decorate with lemon glaze. Mix the icing sugar, lemon juice and water in a bowl. Spread the glaze on the cooled Yam Yams.

You will need

For the pastry
(to make 24 mini quiches)

180g plain white flour
120g butter
1 teaspoon sugar
a pinch of salt
2 tablespoons ice cold water
butter for greasing the tin

For the filling
(enough for 12 mini quiches)

4 rashers/streaky bacon
2 eggs
100ml cream
50g chopped cheese
a pinch of salt and pepper

Tools

weighing scales
large mixing bowl
large measuring jug
airtight plastic bag
table knife
teaspoon
rolling pin
tablespoon, fork
weighing scales
mug, glass or round
    cookie cutter
non-stick cupcake baking tray
    (one for small cupcakes
    works best)

What do you call a pig with no clothes on?
Streaky bacon!

Oh Mais Oui Wee Quiche

To make the pastry

1 Put the flour, sugar and a pinch of salt into a large mixing bowl. Use a table knife to chop the butter into small chunks and then add them to the bowl. Use your fingers to work the butter into the flour until it turns into crumbs.

2 Spoon the cold water into the crumbed flour and butter and mix until it turns into dough. If you find it too sticky, just add a little flour.

3 Place the dough in an airtight plastic bag and chill in the fridge for a couple of hours. Divide the pastry in half. You only need half for the amount of egg filling in this recipe.

4

Flour a large clean work surface area and, using a floured rolling pin, roll out the dough to a thickness of 2cm.

5

Using the rim of a mug or glass or even a round cookie cutter, cut out circles of dough.

6

Grease a baking tray with a little butter. Place the pastry circles individually into each cupcake hole, then chill in the fridge for about 15 minutes.

To make the filling

7

Beat the eggs with a fork in a large measuring jug.

8

Add in the cream and cheese and then season with some salt and pepper.

Repeat the filling ingredients and steps for the other half of the pastry.

9

Ask a grown-up to grill the rashers. Cut the rashers into little bits using a table knife. Spread the bits evenly in the pastry cases and then pour on some egg mixture.

10

Ask a grown-up to preheat the oven to a moderate temperature, 180°C/350°F/gas mark 4. Bake for about 15–20 minutes. Leave them to cool before you eat them.

For other ideas for the leftover pastry, see The Lunchbox Menu, page 61.

45 YUMee

Grandma G's Cheesecake

You will need

For the base
250g digestive biscuits
125g melted butter
1 tablespoon golden syrup

For the filling
225g mascarpone cheese
400g cream cheese
3 eggs
250g castor sugar
1 teaspoon vanilla essence
juice of ½ lemon
rind of ½ lemon

To decorate
icing sugar

Tools
weighing scales
10-inch Springform cake tin
    (tin in which the bottom lifts out)
2 large mixing bowls
wooden spoon
tablespoon
teaspoon
juicer
grater
rolling pin
airtight plastic bag
tea towel
sieve

To make the base

1
Put the butter into a large mixing bowl and, with the help of a grown-up, melt it in the microwave at a low heat for about 3 minutes.

2
Put the biscuits into a plastic bag and squeeze out all of the air. Lay the bag on top of a tea towel on your work surface and then give the plastic bag a few gentle wallops with a rolling pin, crushing all the biscuits.

3
Add the crushed biscuits to the melted butter. Add in the golden syrup and mix well using a wooden spoon.

4
Press the crushed biscuits into the base of your cake tin using the back of a tablespoon. Put the tin into the fridge for about half an hour to set.

To make the filling

5 In a large mixing bowl, cream together the sugar, cream cheese and the mascarpone cheese.

6 Add in the eggs one at a time and mix well with a wooden spoon.

For an extra special treat you could decorate the top of the cake with some whipped cream and blueberries.

7 Add in the lemon rind, lemon juice and the vanilla essence, and mix well.

8 Pour the mixture over the biscuit base in the cake tin.

9 Ask a grown-up to preheat the oven to a moderate temperature, 180°C/ 350°F/gas mark 4. Bake the cake in the oven for about 50 minutes, until the cheesecake is golden brown on top. When the cake is cooked ask the grown-up to remove it from the oven and set aside to cool. Once cooled, it is a good idea to put the cake in the fridge as this helps it to set.

10 Once set, use a sieve to dust a little icing sugar over the top of your cake. Serve it chilled.

For an extra special treat, serve with a scoop of vanilla ice-cream.

Caribbean Fruit Salad

To make the salad

You will need

For the salad
1 pineapple
1 mango
2 kiwis
1 punnet of strawberries

For the mint sugar
a handful of fresh mint
2 dessertspoons sugar

Tools
chopping board
large mixing bowl
safety scissors
pestle and mortar
wooden spoon
table knife

1

Get a grown-up to help you to remove the skin from the pineapple, then use a table knife to carefully chop up the pineapple on a chopping board into bite-size chunks. Place the pineapple chunks into a large mixing bowl.

2

Remove the skin from the mango and slice into bite-size pieces and add these to the pineapple.

3

Remove the skin from the kiwis and slice into bite-size pieces; add these to the pineapple and mango.

4

Wash and halve the strawberries, again using your table knife, and add these to the rest of the fruit.

5

Mix all the fruit together with a wooden spoon.

To make the mint sugar

6

Cut the fresh mint using safety scissors.

7

Using a pestle and mortar, grind the chopped mint and sugar together.

8

Sprinkle the mint sugar on top of the salad and mix well.

9

Chill in the fridge for about 15 minutes to allow the natural flavours to combine. Serve chilled from the fridge.

Rock 'n' Roll Smoothies

You will need the help of a grown-up to use the blender.

Never use a blender without adult supervision.

You will need

1 banana
some fresh strawberries
8 ice cubes
½ cup orange juice
2 heaped dessertspoons
    strawberry yoghurt
1 kiwi fruit

Tools

blender
chopping board
table knife
ice cube tray
dessertspoon
tea cup
serving glass
straw

1 Peel the banana and chop it into bite-size chunks on a chopping board with a table knife.

2  Remove the stems and wash the strawberries. (Keep a little for your garnish.)

3  Remove the ice tray from the freezer and run it under a cold tap, just for a few seconds, this will loosen the ice cubes in the tray and make them easier to take out.

4  Put the ice cubes, banana, strawberries, orange juice and strawberry yoghurt into the blender jug.

If you have a dairy allergy, you could make these using soya yoghurt. Always check with a grown-up first.

You can use any combination of fruit you like. Enjoy your combinations!!!

5

Give the jug to a grown-up and ask them to blend it for a few seconds until all the ice is crushed and all the fruit is combined together.

6

Get the grown-up to pour the smoothie into a large glass.

7

Wash and slice the kiwi and some strawberries and place them on the rim of your glass. Get yourself a nice fat straw and sluuuurp your smoothie.

Gingerbread Men

To make about 16 Gingerbread Men you will need

125g butter
185g light brown sugar
2 tablespoons golden syrup
400g flour
2 teaspoons ground ginger
1 egg

To decorate
tube of writing icing

Tools

2 large mixing bowls
weighing scales, wooden spoon
airtight plastic bag, rolling pin
person-shaped cookie cutter
tablespoon
teaspoon
whisk
sieve
baking paper
baking tray
wire rack

1 Put the butter into a mixing bowl and, with the help of a grown-up, melt it in the microwave at a low heat for about 3 minutes.

2 Add the golden syrup to the melted butter, mix well, then add in sugar and mix well with a wooden spoon.

3 In a separate bowl, beat the egg with a whisk.

4 Slowly add the egg to the butter and sugar mixture. Keep stirring the mixture with a wooden spoon.

5 Sieve the flour and ginger into your mixture. When the mixture becomes too stiff to mix with a wooden spoon, use your fingers. Make sure to put a little flour on your fingers to stop the dough from sticking to them.

6

Shape the dough into a ball. Put the dough ball into an airtight plastic bag and chill in the fridge for about 15 minutes. This makes the dough solid and easier to work.

7

Roll the dough out on a floured surface using a rolling pin. Cut out biscuits about ½ cm thick using your person-shaped cookie cutter.

8

Line a baking tray with baking paper and place each biscuit onto the baking tray, leaving a little space between each one.

9

Ask a grown-up to preheat the oven to a moderate temperature, 180°C/ 350°F/gas mark 4. Bake the biscuits for about 10 minutes. The cooking time really depends on the thickness of the biscuits, the thicker they are the longer they will take. You will know they are ready when they are golden brown.

10

Ask the grown-up to help you place the biscuits on a wire rack to cool.

Decorate your biscuits with writing icing, drawing eyes, a nose, a mouth and buttons.

Homemade Hot Chocolate

You will need the help of a grown-up to warm the milk on the cooker. Never go near a cooker without adult supervision.

To make 4 large mugs you will need

250g good-quality chocolate
   (70% pure cocoa)
1 litre milk
2 dessertspoons sugar
small tub of cream
1 packet of marshmallows

Tools

weighing scales
2 large mixing bowls
large saucepan
dessertspoon, wooden spoon
teaspoons
whisk
large mugs
ladle

1 Break the chocolate into small chunks and put it into a mixing bowl and, with the help of a grown-up, melt the chocolate in the microwave at a low heat for about 3 minutes.

2 With the help of a grown-up, warm the milk in a large saucepan over a very low heat.

3 Add the melted chocolate to the milk and stir with a wooden spoon over the low heat.

4 Add in the sugar and keep mixing.

Yummmmeeeee!!!
Serve each mug with
a teaspoon so you can
scoop up the gooey
marshmallow.

5

Ladle the hot chocolate
into large drinking mugs.

6

In a separate bowl, whisk
some cream until it is light
and fluffy.

7

Add a dollop of cream
and a marshmallow to
each mug.

COCO

Christmas Biscuits

These make great decorations for your tree and a super gift for Santa.

To make about 20 biscuits you will need

200g butter
150g white sugar
250g plain white flour
1 medium egg
½ teaspoon vanilla essence

To decorate

tubes of writing icing
Christmas sprinkles

Tools

weighing scales
large mixing bowl
wooden spoon
sieve, cling film
rolling pin, cookie cutter
baking tray
baking paper
wire rack
top off a tube of toothpaste
pieces of ribbon

1

Put the butter and sugar into a mixing bowl and give them a good mix with a wooden spoon. The mixture should become smooth and creamy with no lumps.

Write Santa's name on the biggest one!!!!

2

Mix the egg and the vanilla essence in with the butter and sugar.

3

Sieve in the flour a little at a time and keep mixing. When the mixture becomes too stiff to mix with a wooden spoon, use your fingers. Make sure to put a little flour on your fingers to stop the dough from sticking to them.

4

Separate the dough in half, press each dough ball into a fat disc with your hands and wrap each half with cling film. Place in the fridge for at least one hour, this makes the dough solid and easier to work.

5

Remove the dough from the fridge and roll it out with a rolling pin on a floured surface to a thickness of about ½ cm.

6

Cut out your shapes, dipping the cutter into flour as you go, and place the biscuit shapes onto a baking tray that has been lined with baking paper. Leave a little room between each biscuit as they will spread out when they cook.

7

To make the hole for the ribbon, cut a small hole out of each biscuit with the clean top off a tube of toothpaste. It's best to cut into the centre of the cookie so that the biscuit won't break.

8

Get a grown-up to preheat the oven to a moderate temperature, 180°C/ 350°F/ gas mark 4. Bake your biscuits for about 10–12 minutes. The cooking time depends on the thickness of the biscuit, the thicker they are the longer they will take. You will know they are ready when they are golden brown.

9

Get a grown-up to help you place the biscuits on a wire rack to cool.

10

Decorate your biscuits with writing icing and decorative Christmas sprinkles. Thread the ribbon through the hole and then hang them on your tree.

YUMee

MENUS

Breakfast 1

Beach Breaky Bickies

For an extra special breakfast treat, here's a great tip. Sandwich a couple of Beach Breaky Bickies together with a yoghurt and fruit filling.

Rock 'n' Roll Smoothies

If you want something other than banana and strawberry smoothies, try this combination: 2 kiwis, 1 mango, 8 ice cubes, ½ cup of natural yoghurt, ½ cup of orange juice and 2 dessertspoons white sugar.

Breakfast 2

Danish Pastries

When making your Danish pastries,
make two rolls and freeze one. When
you want fresh Danishes, take the roll out
of the freezer, leave it to thaw for about 10 minutes and cut using a table knife.
You will find the dough easier to cut when it's still a little frozen.

Caribbean Fruit Salad

If you have a little mint sugar left over from your
Caribbean Fruit Salad, mix it with some whipped cream
and serve over the salad.

Big glass of milk

Lunch

Garlic Bread

Noodle Oodle

Try adding in other vegetables: chopped carrots, broccoli and left-over cold peas.

Eskimo Ices

Different types of fruit – strawberries, blueberries, kiwi – a little grated chocolate or some whipped cream make great toppings for Eskimo Ices.

Lunch Box

Tapas

When making tapas, you don't have to use all the bread at once. The toasted bread will keep in an airtight tin for a couple of days. They are like croutons so try them in soups or salads.

Oh Mais Oui Wee Quiche

When making your quiche, don't throw away the leftover pastry, either make another tray of quiches or freeze the pastry for another time. Some different fillings you could use for your quiches are ham and spring onion, spinach, peas and bacon, garlic salami or different cheeses.

Couscous

Stuff some pita bread with leftover couscous and add a lovely yoghurt dressing. To make the yoghurt dressing, mix natural yoghurt, some crushed garlic and chopped mint together. Great idea for your school lunch box or even for a picnic.

61 YUMee

Birthday Party

Garlic Bread with Cheese

If you like cheesy garlic bread, here's a great tip. At step 6, before you wrap the garlic bread in foil, place a slice of cheese between each slice of bread. This way you get the best gooey, cheesy garlic bread.

Brownies

YUMee Birthday Cake

If you like your Brownies really gooey, here's a great tip. Make some icing. To make the icing, melt 50g of butter and 100g of dark chocolate, add in 2 tablespoons of cream and mix well. Once the Brownies have cooled a little, pour the icing over the top and leave your Brownies aside to set.

Lots of yumeeeee drinks!

Slumber Party

Nachos Muchos Grandes

If you have any salsa left over, don't throw it out. Put it into a bowl and serve on the side as a dip.

Homemade Hot Chocolate

No Bake Belgian Chocolate Cake

Tea Party

To make bite-size scones use the rim of an eggcup to cut out the dough and bake for about ten minutes. Great for a tea party!!!!!

Posh Scones

JAM

Carrot and Orange Muffins

For an extra special treat, here's a great tip!
Ice your carrot and orange muffins with a cream cheese icing. To make the icing, cream together 180g cream cheese and 2 tablespoons of sieved icing sugar, and then just spread a little icing on top of each muffin.

Gingerbread Men